Mrs Magee's
Unusual Plants

by Kelly Gaffney

illustrated by Lauren Mendez

a Capstone company — publishers for children

Engage Literacy is published in the UK by Raintree.
Raintree is an imprint of Capstone Global Library Limited, a company incorporated in England and Wales
having its registered office at 264 Banbury Road, Oxford, OX2 7DY – Registered company number: 6695582

www.raintree.co.uk

Editorial credits
Jennifer Huston, editor; Richard Parker, designer; Katy LaVigne, production specialist

10 9 8 7 6 5 4 3 2 1
Printed and bound in China.

Mrs Magee's Unusual Plants

ISBN: 978 1 4747 3929 0

Contents

Chapter 1
The lost ball

"Oh, Aiden!" cried Olivia.
"That was my new ball!"

"I'm sorry," replied Aiden.
"I didn't mean to kick it so high."

Aiden and Olivia peered
over the old wooden fence.
Olivia's ball lay on the ground
next to an enormous tree.

"Maybe I could climb over the fence
and get it," said Aiden.

"No way!" said Olivia loudly.
"There's something very strange
about that house.
I've never seen anyone going in or out!"

"But I've seen lights in the garden at night," said Aiden.

"Exactly!" replied Olivia.
"Don't you think it's a bit strange?
No one goes in or out,
but there's a spooky green glow
in the back garden at night."

Olivia walked inside, shutting the back door behind her with a crash.

"What's wrong?" asked Mum when she saw Olivia's grumpy face.

"My new ball went over the fence!" grumbled Olivia.

"Well, I'll just take you next door, and we'll ask if we can get it," smiled Mum. "We've been living here for three months now. I think it's time we meet the people who live next door."

"But that house is scary," replied Olivia.

"Don't be silly," laughed Mum.
She took Olivia's hand
and walked to the front door.

"Wait for me," called Aiden.
"I'm coming, too!"

Mum, Olivia and Aiden walked up the hill to the house next door.

There were tall weeds everywhere, and paint was coming off the sides of the house.

When they got to the front door, Mum rang the bell.

DING-DONG! DING-DONG!

Olivia and Aiden hid behind Mum, but there was no answer.

Mum tried again.
DING-DONG! DING-DONG!

"I can hear something inside,"
said Aiden quietly.

Chapter 2
Who lives next door?

Slowly the big wooden door opened.
Olivia and Aiden gasped.

"Hello," said a little voice from inside.
"Can I help you?"

"Hi," said Mum.
"My name is Lucy, and I live next door.
These are my children, Olivia and Aiden."

Olivia and Aiden peered out
from behind Mum and saw
a little old woman in a wheelchair.

"Hello," they both said quietly.

"We're very sorry to bother you," said Mum. "But the children's ball went over the fence into your garden. Do you mind if we get it?"

"Of course not," smiled the old woman.
"Please, come in.
My name is Mrs Magee.
Please excuse my garden.
It's a mess.
I find it hard to do some things
in this wheelchair."

When they got to the back door
of the house, Aiden saw the ball
beside the tree.
He ran outside to get it.
As he picked up the ball,
he saw a building off the back of the house.
He quickly ran back to Mum.

Chapter 3
The greenhouse

"Excuse me, Mrs Magee, but what's that?"
asked Aiden, pointing to the building
in the garden.
"Olivia and I have seen a light coming
from there at nighttime."

"Oh," smiled Mrs Magee.
"That's my greenhouse.
That's where I keep my hungry little friends."

Olivia and Aiden looked frightened.
Mrs Magee saw their faces and laughed.
"Oh, don't be scared," she said.
"There's nothing in my greenhouse
except plants.
But the plants I collect are very special."

"Why?" asked the children.

"Because my plants eat insects,"
replied Mrs Magee.
"Would you like to see them?"

"Yes, please!" said Olivia and Aiden together.

"I'd love to see them, too," said Mum.

"Then follow me," said Mrs Magee.
"The greenhouse is attached
to the side of the house.
It makes it easier for me to get
in and out with my wheelchair."

Mrs Magee rolled her chair back through
the house as the children and Mum followed.
When they came to a doorway,
Mrs Magee pushed open the door
to the greenhouse.
They all went inside.

"Wow!" the children shouted.

Inside the greenhouse were
lots of long tables, covered with pots
of all shapes and sizes.
Mrs Magee wheeled her chair
up to one of the tables.

"It's hard for me to dig in the garden,"
she explained.
"So I started collecting these unusual plants.
I keep them in pots so I can
do my gardening from my wheelchair."

"What a fantastic idea!" said Mum.

Chapter 4
Mrs Magee's unusual plants

Mrs Magee picked up one of the little pots
and showed the children the plant.
"This is a Venus flytrap," she said.
"It catches flies with its leaves."
She moved across to another table.
"This one is a pitcher plant.
It catches insects swimming in the water
inside its leaves."

The children stared at the plants
with their eyes open wide in surprise.
"Are they dangerous?" asked Aiden.

"Only if you're an insect!" laughed
Mrs Magee.

"Your plants are very interesting, Mrs Magee," said Olivia.

"I'm glad you like them," replied Mrs Magee. "Sadly, I don't get many visitors these days. It's nice to be able to share them with someone.
Would you and Aiden
each like a plant to take home?
I have so many, and they're very easy to look after."

Olivia and Aiden both looked up at Mum.
"I'm sure the children would love that, Mrs Magee," smiled Mum.
"Thank you so much.
It's been lovely meeting you."

"Yes, thank you very much, Mrs Magee," said Olivia and Aiden together.

"It was really nice of Mrs Magee to give each of us a special plant," Olivia said as they walked home. "Maybe we could give her some plums from our garden."

"That's a great idea, Olivia!" said Mum. "I think she would really like that."

"And maybe we could help out in her garden and greenhouse, too!" said Aiden.

"I think Mrs Magee would enjoy that, too," smiled Mum.